READ-TO-ME
TREASURY

❦ VOLUME ONE ❧

DISNEY
PRESS

NEW YORK

All books illustrated by the storybook artists at Disney Publishing Worldwide.

CONTENTS

❦ INTRODUCTION ❦

Meet Bambi and friends in the forest; dine with a talkative teapot at the Beast's castle; listen to a concert in an underwater palace; take a ride in a pumpkin carriage . . . You and your child can share these magical adventures and more in this treasury of beloved Disney tales.

Dear Parents and Caregivers:

Educators will tell you that reading aloud for at least fifteen minutes a day is one of the best gifts you can give your child. Not only will you help your child develop language skills, but you will be setting the foundation for a love of books and a desire to read. You will also be spending time with your loved one. What could be better than that?

The Whens and Whys of Reading Aloud

You can read aloud to your child whenever you have the time or whenever your child hands you a book and says, "Please read to me." Bedtime and naptime make a nice routine time for reading. But don't forget to take along a book when you visit the pediatrician or dentist. Reading can be a comforting diversion. For trips on a plane, bus, or train, reading can help pass the time.

Depending on the age of your child, he or she might want to sit with this treasury and flip through the pages, talk aloud to the characters, or raise questions about what happens on a particular page. Let your child experience the book in his or her own way. Be around to answer or comment. The more you and your child become involved with the story, the more an appreciation for books, language, and storytelling will grow.

You might ask your child to choose which of the stories he or she would like to hear. Don't be surprised if after reading one tale your child asks you to reread that same tale again and yet again. Revisiting stories helps young children make connections between the stories they hear and the pictures and words they see. They begin to be able to predict what is going to happen next. Familiarity makes your child an expert—a positive feeling that is then attached to the whole reading experience. Repetition not only helps children develop a comfort zone with books, but it also reinforces important letter- and word-recognition skills.

If your child shows an interest in words, you might pause at certain places in the text and ask: Can you find the word *dinglehopper*? Can you find the names of the Seven Dwarfs? Associating written words with storytelling is an important reading-readiness skill. But remember to let your child set the pace and tell you what he or she wants to learn or talk about.

Quick Tips

Here are some hints to help you and your little reader on your way:

• Set a reading mood. Let your little listener settle in and, perhaps by looking over the cover, start thinking about the story.

• Children have different attention spans. Note that each of the stories in the treasury is divided into sections, so you have a natural place to stop and then start again at another sitting.

• Put lots of expression into your reading—if possible, change your voice to fit each character.

• Keep your child involved. Invite him or her to turn the pages when it's time.

• At the end of each section, you might raise questions such as: What do you think will happen to Simba? Will he become the Lion King? Will the Beast ever free Belle? Why do you think so? Do you think the Little Mermaid will obey her father? Never pry an interpretation from your child. Let your child's interests be your guide.

• Don't rush. A slow-paced read gives your child time to explore the pictures and make their own mental map of what's happening in the story. Plus, it reinforces the message that you enjoy spending quiet time together.

So now it's time to find that cozy nook, to cuddle and snuggle with your child, and to share a Disney read-to-me story together. You're ready to embark on the magical road of reading!

The Editors

WALT DISNEY'S

Snow White
and the Seven Dwarfs

 RETOLD BY LIZA BAKER

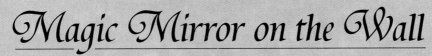

Magic Mirror on the Wall

Once upon a time, there lived a beautiful princess named Snow White. Her stepmother, the Queen, was jealous of Snow White's beauty.

Every day the Queen would ask, "Magic mirror on the wall, who is the fairest one of all?"

Each time the mirror would answer, "You are."

But one day the mirror replied, "A lovely maid I see, who is more fair than thee."

"It's Snow White!" snarled the Queen.

At that moment, Snow White was in the
courtyard singing as she went about her chores.
    A handsome young prince was riding by and
heard her lovely voice. He climbed the castle wall to
find her. Shy Snow White ran up to her balcony.

13

From the courtyard below, the Prince sang to
Snow White. She listened happily to his song, and
did not see the evil queen watching them.

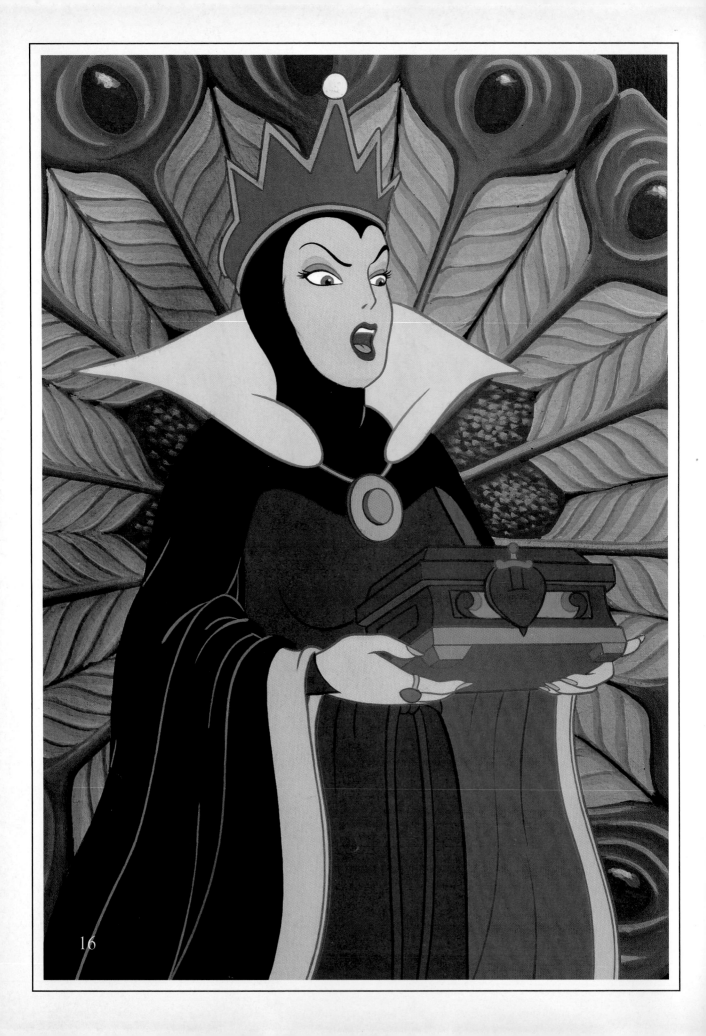

Enraged with jealousy, the Queen ordered her huntsman, "Take Snow White into the forest and kill her."

The huntsman led Snow White deep into the woods, but he could not harm her. "I can't do as the Queen wishes!" he wept. "Run away, child, and never come back!"

Snow White fled into the forest. As she ran, she felt haunting eyes watching her. The trees seemed to reach out to grab her.

With nowhere left to run, she fell to the ground and began to cry.

In the midst of her tears, Snow White looked up and found herself surrounded by forest animals. "Do you know where I can stay?" she asked them.

23

The friendly animals led Snow White to a tiny cottage in the woods.

"It's like a doll's house!" said Snow White. She knocked at the door but no one answered. "May I come in?" she called. Slowly she stepped inside.

As Snow White wandered through the house she discovered seven little chairs and seven little beds.

"Seven little children must live here! Let's clean the house and surprise them," the Princess suggested. "Then maybe they'll let me stay."

The Seven Dwarfs

Close by, the seven dwarfs who owned the cottage were busy working in their mine. All day long they dug for jewels.

At five o'clock it was time to go. Doc led Grumpy, Happy, Sleepy, Sneezy, Bashful, and Dopey home, singing and whistling as they went.

When the dwarfs reached their cottage the light was on—someone was in their house! They crept inside and tiptoed upstairs to find Snow White fast asleep beneath their blankets.

"It's a monster!" whispered one dwarf.

Stepping closer, Doc cried out, "Why, it's a girl!"
Snow White sat up and said, "How do you do?"
She explained to the dwarfs who she was and
what the evil queen had planned for her. "Don't
send me away," she begged.

"If you let me stay, I'll wash and sew and sweep
and cook," Snow White promised.

At that the dwarfs shouted, "Hooray! She stays!"
And the happy princess ran to the kitchen to
prepare dinner.

36

The dwarfs rushed downstairs to eat, but Snow White said, "Supper is not quite ready. You'll just have time to wash."

"Wash?" cried the bewildered dwarfs.

All the dwarfs but one headed to the tub. "I'd like to see anybody make *me* wash!" said Grumpy.

Just as Grumpy spoke, the other dwarfs pounced on him and dumped him into the tub. They scrubbed him squeaky-clean. "You'll pay for this!" growled Grumpy.

40

Back at the castle, the Queen asked the mirror once again, "Who is the fairest in the land?"

"Snow White," answered the mirror. Then it revealed where the Princess was hiding.

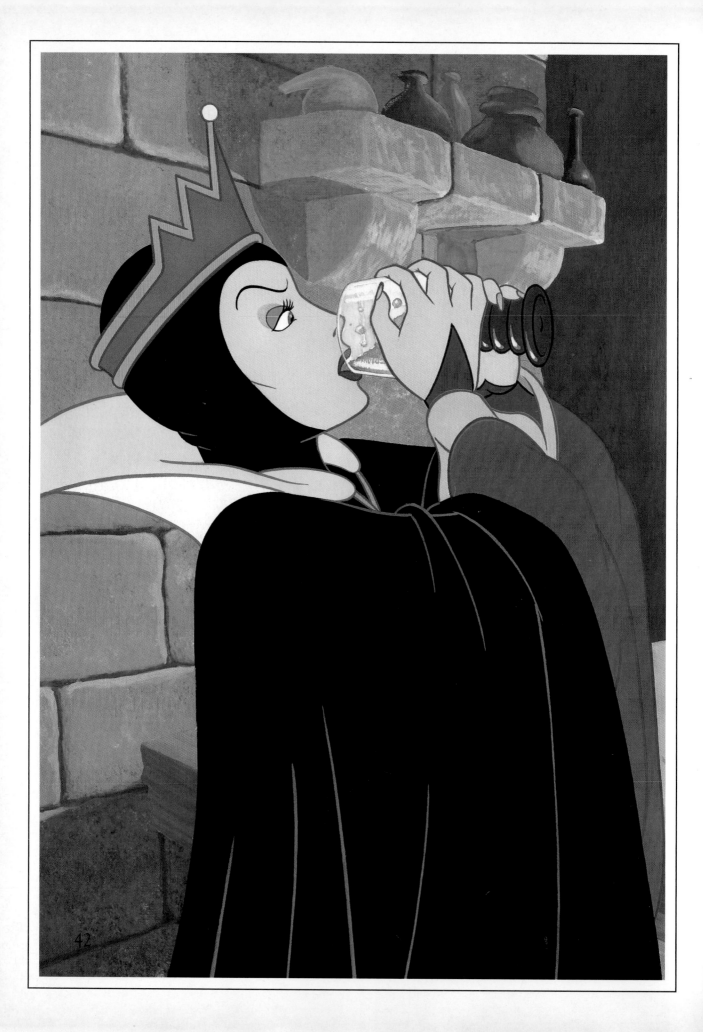

The angry queen drank a potion that disguised her as an old hag. Then she created a magic apple. "With one bite of this poisoned apple, Snow White's eyes will close forever," she cackled. The only cure for the sleeping spell was love's first kiss.

Unaware of the Queen's plot,
Snow White and the Seven Dwarfs
sang and danced late into the night.

The next morning, Snow
White kissed each dwarf good-bye
as he marched off toward the mine.
Doc warned the Princess, "The
Queen is a sly one. Beware of strangers!"

The Sleeping Spell

From the shadows of the trees, the Queen watched the dwarfs leave. Slowly, she crept up to the cottage.

"All alone, my pet?" the disguised queen asked
Snow White. Then she offered the poisoned apple.
"Go on, dearie. Have a bite."

51

Several birds recognized the wicked queen and knocked the apple from her hands. But Snow White felt sorry for the old woman and helped her inside the cottage.

Sensing danger, the forest animals ran off to warn the dwarfs. But it was too late.

Snow White bit into the poisoned fruit!

Dropping the apple, Snow White fell to the ground. "Now I'll be the fairest in the land!" cackled the Queen.

57

Lightning flashed and thunder cracked as the Queen fled from the cottage.

But before she could escape, the Seven Dwarfs came charging at her.

"There she goes!" cried Grumpy. "After her!"

The dwarfs chased the Queen to the top of a rocky cliff.

"I'll fix you!" she shrieked, as she tried to roll an enormous boulder down on top of them.

60

Suddenly, a bolt of lighting struck the
ledge where the Queen stood!
    The rock crumbled beneath her feet and
the evil queen tumbled off the mountaintop
and into the darkness below.

64

The heartbroken dwarfs built a coffin for Snow White and watched over her day and night. Then one day the Prince appeared.

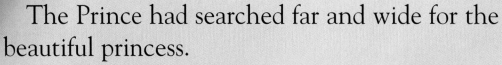

The Prince had searched far and wide for the beautiful princess.

With great sorrow, he kissed Snow White farewell.

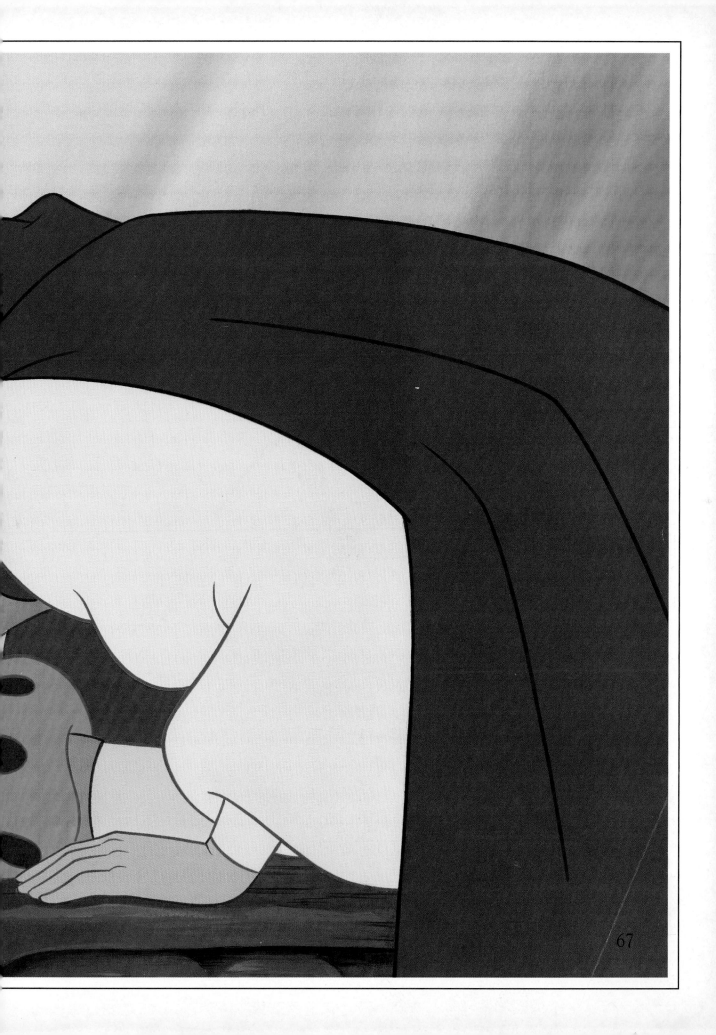

Slowly, Snow White began to awaken. The Prince's kiss had broken the spell! The dwarfs cheered and hugged one another joyously.

Snow White thanked the dwarfs for all they had done, then kissed each one good-bye. Together, the Prince and Snow White rode off to his castle, where they lived happily ever after.

Bambi

RETOLD BY LIZA BAKER

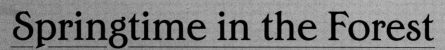

Springtime in the Forest

Deep in the forest, Thumper the bunny was spreading exciting news. "A new prince is born!" he shouted.

In a nearby clearing, a mama deer lay with her newborn son.

"This is quite an occasion," said Friend Owl. "It isn't every day a prince is born."

The mama deer named her son Bambi.

Days passed and Bambi began to explore his world. There was so much to see!

"Good morning," called some possums. Bambi turned his head upside down to greet them!

Then a furry creature popped out of the ground. "Good morning!" said the mole. Startled, Bambi tumbled to the ground.

Thumper called out, "Get up! Try again!" Bambi struggled to his feet. He didn't want to miss any of the fun!

Every day Bambi's friends showed him new
things. "Those are birds," they explained.
"Burr!" repeated Bambi.
"It's burr-duh," corrected Thumper.
"Bird!" said Bambi loudly. The bunnies cheered.

"Bird!" said Bambi again when a butterfly landed on his tail.

Thumper laughed. "No, that's a butterfly!"

Then Thumper introduced his friend to flowers. But as Bambi bent toward them he found himself nose-to-nose with a skunk! "Flower," said Bambi proudly. Thumper giggled, but "Flower" was that little skunk's name from then on.

85

When thunder rumbled, Bambi hurried to his cozy thicket. As he nestled close to his mother, the pitter-patter of rain lulled him to sleep.

Later, sunshine filled the sky again and Bambi's mother decided it was time to show him the meadow.

The meadow was so open and green that Bambi
darted forward. But his mother leaped in front of him.
"There may be danger!" she scolded.

Once Bambi's mother was sure it was safe, Bambi
bounded into the field. Suddenly, he heard a "Rrribit!"

Bambi followed the frog until it splashed into a
nearby pond. Then Bambi noticed his own reflection
and that of a smiling girl fawn.

"That's little Faline," Bambi's mother told him. "Go on. Say hello."

"Hello," he said shyly. Faline giggled and began to chase him. Bambi joined in the game and they played happily in the field. Bambi had found a new friend.

The Great Prince

A thundering herd of stags galloped onto the meadow. The biggest stag stopped and looked at Bambi. Bambi asked his mother who the stag was. She answered, "He is very brave and wise. He is the Great Prince of the Forest." He was also Bambi's father.

95

Suddenly a gunshot sounded! As the animals scattered, Bambi lost his mother. Instantly, the Great Prince was at Bambi's side. He reunited Bambi with his mother and led them home safely.

Time passed quickly in the forest, and Bambi woke one morning to find the world covered in a soft white blanket. It was his first winter!

Bambi found Thumper skating on the frozen pond. "Come on, Bambi!" Thumper called.

Bambi ran toward the ice. With a sudden *splat*, Bambi slipped onto his belly. And when Thumper tried to teach him how to balance on the ice, Bambi slid them both into a snowbank!

They landed by a small den where Flower lay sleeping. Flower explained that skunks sleep through the winter. "Good night," he murmured.

The snowy days seemed endless, and food grew scarce. "I'm hungry, Mother," said Bambi.

"Winter won't last forever," she assured him.

Finally, Bambi saw the first sign of spring—a small patch of grass. Bambi was nibbling at it when a gunshot rang out!

"Run for the thicket!" cried his mother.

Bambi ran as fast as he could. When he reached the thicket he said, "We made it, Mother!" But she wasn't there. Then Bambi heard a second gunshot.

As Bambi cried, the Great Prince appeared before him. "Your mother can't be with you anymore," he said gently. "Come with me, my son." Together, Bambi and his father walked deeper into the forest.

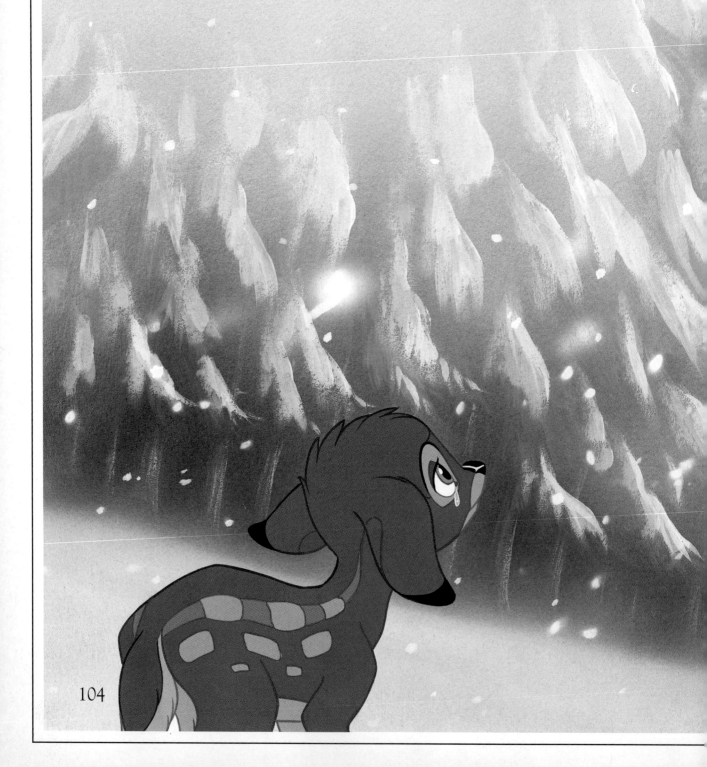

Before long, flowers began to bloom and birds' songs filled the air. Even Flower awakened from his long winter's sleep. Spring had arrived!

During the winter, Bambi had grown into a handsome buck. And Thumper and Flower had both grown to their full sizes.

When Friend Owl saw them, he said, "It won't be long before you're twitterpated. Nearly everyone falls in love in the springtime." The three friends declared that it would not happen to them!

111

But when Flower saw a pretty skunk, he happily walked off with her. Then Thumper came across a lovely bunny. When she petted his ears, Thumper's foot went *thump*, *thump*, *thump*.

Feeling lonely, Bambi stopped to drink from a pond. A familiar face looked back at him in the reflection.

"Don't you remember me?" asked a sweet voice. "I'm Faline." Faline the fawn had grown into a beautiful doe!

Together, Bambi and Faline played in the meadow just as they had done the summer before.

Now Bambi understood what Friend Owl meant. He had never felt so happy.

Suddenly an angry stag appeared. "Help!" cried Faline as the stag tried to force her to come with him. Bambi butted the stag with all his strength.

The defeated stag limped away, and from that day on Bambi and Faline were inseparable.

Man Comes to the Forest

Bambi awoke one morning sensing danger. Smoke was in the air and he could see a fire burning.

The Great Prince told him, "It is Man. We must go deep into the forest. Hurry!"

119

News of the danger quickly spread. Frightened
animals scurried underground or raced deeper
into the forest.

121

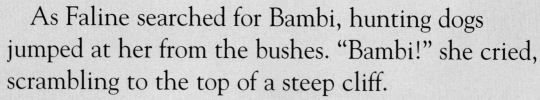

As Faline searched for Bambi, hunting dogs jumped at her from the bushes. "Bambi!" she cried, scrambling to the top of a steep cliff.

The hounds snapped at her heels, barking ferociously. Faline was trapped!

122

124

Just then, Bambi sprang out of the woods and charged the dogs with his sharp antlers.

He attacked one dog after another until Faline bounded to safety.

Bambi escaped the dogs but as he leaped after Faline, a gunshot sounded. Wounded, Bambi tumbled to the ground. Fire raged toward him but he couldn't get up. Then he heard the voice of the Great Prince.

128

"You must get up, Bambi," said the Great Prince. Bambi staggered to his feet. "Follow me," his father said. "We'll be safe in the river."

130

Soon they came to a waterfall. With nowhere else to turn, they leaped toward the rapids below.

Bambi and the Great Prince finally reached the island where Faline stood waiting. Even as they watched the beautiful forest burn, they all knew that when Man was gone, the animals would bravely rebuild their homes.

Autumn turned to cold white winter and then to spring. "Wake up, Friend Owl!" said Thumper and his four thumping baby bunnies.

"It's happened!" called Flower to the baby skunk scurrying behind him.

The animals circled around the thicket where Faline and her two fawns lay.

"Prince Bambi ought to be mighty proud," said the owl as the fawns opened their big eyes to greet their friendly visitors.

Bambi was now the Prince of the Forest. And as he and his family began their lives together, Bambi thought of the lessons he hoped to teach his children — lessons he had learned from his mother and father long ago.

WALT DISNEY'S

Cinderella

 RETOLD BY DELLA COHEN

Once upon a time...

Long ago in a faraway land, poor Cinderella lived with her mean stepfamily. They filled her days with cooking, scrubbing, washing, and chores of every kind.

140

Cinderella's stepmother and two stepsisters, Anastasia and Drizella, never helped with her work. But Cinderella remained cheerful and kind.

She made friends with all the animals that she met.

143

Cinderella even made clothes for the mice who shared her small attic room.

One day, Jaq, her favorite mouse, was upset.

"What's all the fuss about?" Cinderella asked. Jaq led her to a new mouse that was caught in a trap!

Cinderella quickly freed the frightened mouse.
Then she dressed him in new clothes and found
the perfect name for him: Gus.

147

When it was time for Cinderella to feed the chickens, the mice headed for the barnyard. Cinderella always saved some corn for them.

But today, the mean old cat, Lucifer, blocked their way. Jaq was chosen to get the cat to chase him. Then the other mice could scoot outside.

The plan worked. Jaq kicked the cat and angry Lucifer began chasing him.

But Jaq was too fast for Lucifer and made it safely into a mousehole. While Lucifer waited for Jaq to come out, the other mice scampered by him!

151

Cinderella spent the rest of her day attending to chores.

"Take that ironing," Drizella demanded.

"Don't forget the mending," Anastasia added.

"Pick up the laundry and get on with your duties," her stepmother ordered.

Meanwhile, at the royal palace, the King complained to the Grand Duke. "It's high time my son got married," he sobbed. "I want grandchildren!"

The King decided to hold a ball. "If all the eligible maidens come," said the King, "the Prince is bound to find his bride among them."

The Royal Ball

Later that day, Cinderella heard a knock on the door. "Open in the name of the King," said the royal messenger. He handed Cinderella an invitation.

When her stepmother read the invitation aloud, Drizella and Anastasia became excited. Each imagined the Prince falling in love with her.

Cinderella was also excited. "Why, that means I can go, too!" she said. The stepsisters laughed. "Every eligible maiden is supposed to attend," answered Cinderella.

Surprisingly, her stepmother agreed. "I don't see why you can't go . . . *if* you get all your work done, and *if* you can find something suitable to wear."

Cinderella raced to her room and found a dress that had belonged to her mother. With a little stitching, she could make it pretty.

As Cinderella worked on the dress, her stepmother and stepsisters called for her and gave her many chores. "Get them done quickly," said her stepmother.

When Cinderella had to put the dress aside, her animal friends began to work on it. They gathered beads and a sash that the stepsisters had thrown away.

Soon they had created a beautiful gown!

Cinderella finally finished her chores and
went to her room. Then she realized it was too
late to get ready for the ball. She was so sad!

Suddenly, the mice yelled, "Surprise!"

They showed Cinderella the beautiful gown.
"Oh, thank you so much!" she cried.

Cinderella put on the gown and hurried to join her stepfamily. But when her jealous stepsisters recognized their old sash and beads, they tore Cinderella's gown to shreds!

Cinderella's friends watched sadly as she wept in the garden. "It's no use," she sobbed. "Nothing will help."

At that moment, bright, sparkling lights began floating and swirling around Cinderella.

Poof! Cinderella's Fairy Godmother appeared. "Dry those tears," she told Cinderella. "You can't go to the ball looking like that."

"But I'm not going," said Cinderella.

"Of course you are," replied the Fairy Godmother.

171

She waved her magic wand over a pumpkin, and a regal coach appeared!

"Oh, it's beautiful," said Cinderella. The Fairy Godmother waved her wand again.

Jaq and Gus and two other mice turned into
four beautiful white horses. Then she changed
Major the horse into the coach driver and Bruno
the dog into the footman.

Next, the Fairy Godmother turned Cinderella's torn dress into a beautiful gown. In a flash, there were also tiny glass slippers for her feet.

"On the stroke of midnight, the spell will be broken," the Fairy Godmother warned. "Everything will be as before."

The Glass Slipper

The ball was just beginning when Cinderella arrived. She climbed the long staircase. *Oh, how happy I am*, she thought.

The King and the Grand Duke watched as the maidens walked forward to meet the Prince. The Prince was unimpressed with them all.

Then he noticed Cinderella.

Entranced, he walked past all of the other maidens, and led Cinderella into the ballroom.

They began to dance.

They danced every
dance until . . . the clock
began to strike midnight.
Bong! Bong!

"I must go!" Cinderella cried in a panic, freeing her hand from the Prince's. As she fled, she lost a glass slipper on the staircase.

The clock sounded as the coach raced from the palace. It was midnight!

The horses were mice again.
Cinderella was in rags. But she
still had one glass slipper.

The next morning, the Prince proclaimed that he would marry the girl who had lost her slipper at the ball.

"Find her!" roared the King. The Grand Duke would check every house in the kingdom for a maiden whose foot fit the glass slipper.

Cinderella was so happy! She eagerly awaited the Grand Duke's visit.

No matter what Drizella and Anastasia ordered Cinderella to do, she nodded dreamily. Cinderella's stepfamily could not understand the reason for her joy.

Then, the wicked
stepmother realized that
it must have been
Cinderella who was the
Prince's favorite at the
ball!

She locked Cinderella
in her room.

"Let me out!" Cinderella cried.

But her stepmother put the key in her pocket, laughing her meanest laugh.

Then Cinderella heard a knock at the front door. The Grand Duke had arrived!

Meanwhile, Jaq and Gus had seen what the stepmother did. They took the key out of her pocket, and slipped it under Cinderella's door.

Downstairs, the Grand Duke watched his footman try to squeeze Anastasia's big foot into the slipper. Of course, the slipper did not fit Drizella, either.

As she hurried down the steps, Cinderella heard the Grand Duke ask, "Are there any other maidens in the house?"

"Please wait!" called Cinderella. "May I try on the slipper?"

The angry stepmother tripped the footman as he approached Cinderella. The glass slipper shattered. "Oh, no!" moaned the Grand Duke.

"But you see," said Cinderella, reaching into her pocket, "I have the other slipper." Quickly, the Grand Duke put the slipper on Cinderella's foot.

It fit perfectly! Cinderella was the Prince's love!

Cinderella married the Prince and lived happily ever after. And so did Jaq, Gus, and all of Cinderella's animal friends!

THE LITTLE MERMAID

 RETOLD BY AMY EDGAR

Daydreams

Under the sea, merfolk hurried toward King Triton's palace. Everyone wanted a good seat for the concert.

207

The merfolk watched as Sebastian, the court composer, signaled for the music to begin. Six of King Triton's daughters sang and swirled around the stage to the sounds of the underwater orchestra.

Tonight King Triton's youngest daughter, Ariel, would sing her first solo. But when the giant clamshell opened, Ariel was nowhere to be seen.

"Ariel!" bellowed King Triton.

Nearby, Ariel had forgotten all about the concert. She and her friend Flounder were swimming around a sunken ship. Ariel loved looking for things from the human world above.

"It's wonderful!" she cried, finding a shiny fork.

"D-d-did you hear something?" asked Flounder.
"You're not getting cold fins, are you?" teased
Ariel.
Then Flounder spotted a large, dark shape
swimming right toward them! "Shark!" he yelled.

216

The two friends swam as fast as they could, but the shark could swim faster. So Ariel whisked Flounder through a small hole in an anchor. The hungry shark followed them and got stuck.

"Take that, you big bully!" Flounder jeered.

Ariel brought her new treasure to Scuttle, the seagull. "This is a dinglehopper," explained Scuttle, combing his feathers with the fork. "Humans use these to straighten their hair."

Deep below, the Sea Witch, Ursula, was gazing into her magic bubble, spying on Ariel.

Suddenly, Ariel remembered the concert! She hurried home to find King Triton waiting for her. He was angry about the ruined concert, but even angrier when he learned of Ariel's trip to the surface.

"Never go to the surface again!" he ordered.

Later, the King told Sebastian, "Ariel needs supervision, and you are just the crab to do it."

Meanwhile, Ariel was daydreaming in her secret grotto. "I don't see how a world that makes such wonderful things could be bad," she said.

The Prince

Ariel looked up and saw the shadow of a ship overhead. She swam to the surface to get a closer look. There, she saw a handsome young man. The other humans called him Prince Eric.

"Hurricane a-comin'!" a sailor shouted.

Howling wind tore at the ship's sails. Giant waves tossed it onto the jagged rocks. Prince Eric was thrown into the ocean!

Ariel frantically searched for the Prince. Finding him, she needed all her strength for the rescue.

Safe on the shore, Ariel sang to the unconscious Prince. At last, he began to awaken. "Someday, I'll be part of your world," she said, slipping into the sea.

Minutes later, the Prince's servant, Sir Grimsby, discovered him. "A girl rescued me," said the Prince groggily. "And she had the most beautiful voice."

When King Triton found out that Ariel had been up to the surface again, he flew into a rage!

"Humans are all the same!" King Triton shouted. "Savage fish eaters, incapable of any feeling!" With a few strokes of his trident, he destroyed all of Ariel's treasures, and swam off.

233

Two sinister eels interrupted Ariel's sobbing. "We were sent by someone," they hissed, "who can make all your dreams come true."

The eels brought Ariel to Ursula. The Sea Witch was willing to help Ariel—in exchange for her voice!

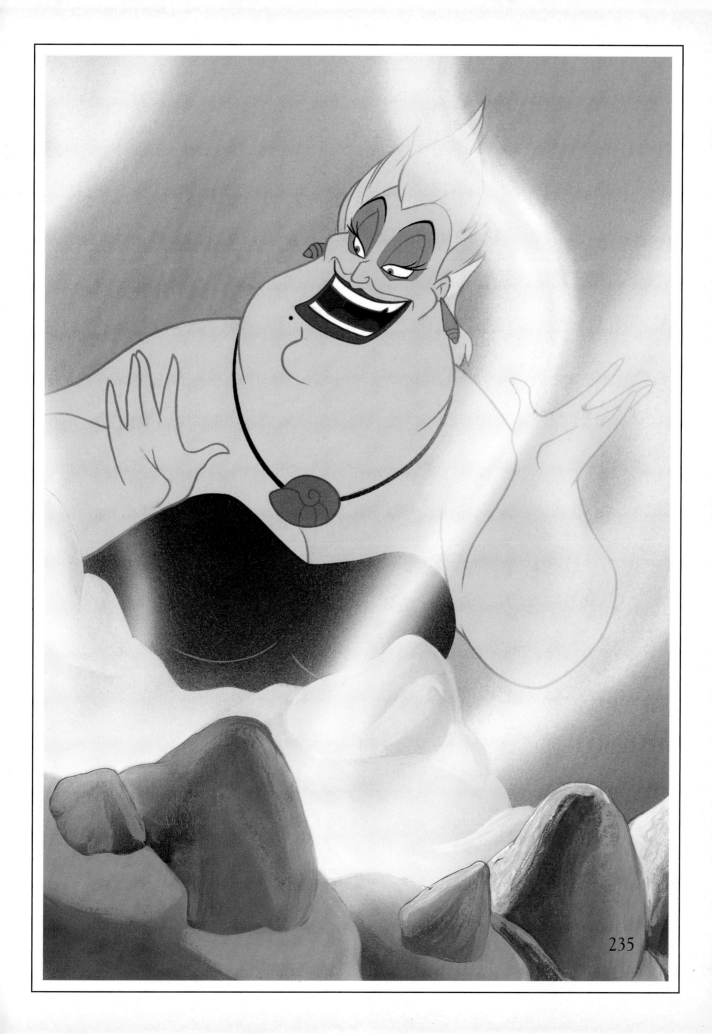

"But," Ursula added, "the Prince must fall in love with you by sunset on the third day." If not, Ariel would change back into a mermaid and become Ursula's slave forever!

The ocean churned as Ariel's voice was captured inside a magical shell and her tail turned into legs.

Prince Eric and his dog, Max, found Ariel on the beach. "You seem very familiar to me," said Eric. "Have we met?" Ariel could only nod.

"Don't worry, I'll help you." He smiled. Although she looked like the girl who rescued him, Eric didn't think it could be her. She couldn't speak, much less sing!

That evening, Ariel appeared for dinner in a pretty gown. To the Prince's surprise, Ariel picked up her fork and began combing her hair, just as Scuttle had taught her!

Under the sea, a worried King Triton had not been able to find Ariel. "Leave no shell unturned until she's safe at home!" he told his servants.

Meanwhile, Ariel and Eric were happily rowing on a lagoon. Just as they were about to kiss, Ursula's eels overturned the boat!

Ursula's Plan

Ursula hatched a plan to keep Eric from falling in love with Ariel. She turned herself into a pretty girl named Vanessa, and she wore the shell containing Ariel's voice.

That evening, the Prince heard someone singing.
It was the voice of the girl who had saved him!
Eric looked out to see Vanessa. He fell under her
wicked spell.

247

When Ariel awoke the next morning, she saw Eric with Vanessa. "The wedding ship departs at sunset," the Prince told Grimsby.

Now Ariel had lost her chance at true love and was doomed to be Ursula's slave forever!

Aboard the wedding ship, Vanessa cackled, "Triton's daughter will be mine!"

Looking through the porthole, Scuttle saw the mirror reveal that Vanessa was really Ursula. He quickly found Ariel. "The Prince is marrying the Sea Witch in disguise!" he exclaimed.

"Find a way to stall that wedding!" Sebastian yelled to Scuttle as they took off to rescue Eric. Flounder helped Ariel along, but the sun was starting to set. There wasn't much time left!

Scuttle and his friends did their best to interrupt the wedding.

"Why you little . . ." Vanessa yelled, trying to defend herself.

In all the commotion, the magic shell shattered to the ground just as Ariel reached the ship.

"Eric?" Ariel spoke.

"You can talk!" said the Prince. "You're the one! It was you all the time."

Happy at last, the Prince leaned over to kiss Ariel.
But seconds before their lips met, the sun set.

"You're too late!" shouted Ursula, turning into her
beastly self. Ariel found her legs changed back into a
mermaid's tail.

"It's not you I'm after," Ursula told Ariel, whisking her into the sea. "I've got much bigger fish to fry." At those words, King Triton appeared.

Ursula told him about the deal she had made with Ariel. In return for his daughter's freedom, the King agreed to take Ariel's place as a slave.

261

"At last, this is mine," Ursula laughed, placing Triton's crown on her head. Using her new powers, Ursula grew to a monstrous size. "Now I am the ruler of all the ocean!"

But the brave prince steered a ship over the raging waves right toward Ursula! The bow of the ship pierced her cold heart. Slowly, Ursula's horrendous body sank beneath the waves.

All at once, the ocean was calm and King Triton's power was restored. Now he realized how much Eric and Ariel loved each other. He changed Ariel's tail back into legs.

"I love you, Daddy," said Ariel, hugging him. He knew he would miss her terribly.

All the merfolk and sea creatures gathered to watch the happy couple's wedding. Everyone cheered as Eric kissed his new princess. Then they sailed away to live happily ever after.

Disney's
Beauty and the Beast

✿ RETOLD BY ELLEN TITLEBAUM ✿

THE SPELL IS CAST

One winter's eve, a beggar offered the Prince a red rose in return for shelter. He sneered at her gift, and turned her away.

"Do not be deceived by appearances," the beggar warned, revealing that she was an enchantress!

The Enchantress turned the Prince into a hideous
beast, and placed a spell on everyone in the castle. She
left behind only the rose she had offered him.

For the spell to be broken, the Prince would have to love another and earn that person's love in return before the rose's last petal fell.

Belle lived in a village near the castle. She loved to read books about adventure and romance.

One morning, Gaston the hunter saw Belle and boasted, "That's the girl I'm going to marry."

At Belle's house, her father, Maurice, was working on a new invention.

"You'll win first prize at the fair tomorrow," predicted Belle.

But Maurice and his horse Philippe never made it to the fair. They became lost in the dark forest.

Black bats flew out of the shadows, followed by growling wolves. The terrified horse threw his rider off and charged into the woods.

Maurice ran down a hillside, crashing into branches and toppling over gigantic roots until he saw an old gate in front of a castle.

He forced the gate open and escaped just before the wolves reached him!

Maurice approached the castle, and stepped inside. "Not a word," whispered Cogsworth, the clock, to Lumiere, the candelabrum. The people in the castle had been changed into enchanted objects!

Friendly Lumiere announced, "Welcome, Monsieur!"

Suddenly, a huge beast stormed into the room.
"A stranger!" the Beast growled.

Huge, clawed hands grabbed Maurice and
took him to the dungeon!

At that very moment, Gaston had arrived at Belle's house to propose marriage. A crowd waited outside to celebrate.

"Say you'll marry me," he ordered. Belle refused. She did not like the conceited bully!

When the crowd had left, Philippe arrived, with no rider.

"Philippe! Where's Papa? You must take me to him!" cried Belle.

292

BELLE'S PROMISE

Belle rode through the forest, braving the thick fog and frightening sounds. Soon she saw the huge turrets and gates of the castle rising out of the mist.

When Belle entered the castle, she found her
father locked in the dungeon. As they embraced,
a voice boomed from the shadows.

294

"I am the master of this castle!" roared the Beast.

"Take me instead," Belle cried.

When Belle promised to stay with the Beast forever, he released Maurice.

296

297

The Beast showed Belle to her room. "You can go anywhere you like . . . except the west wing. You'll join me for dinner," said the Beast and then he was gone.

Belle was angry at the Beast's unkind treatment. Not even Mrs. Potts, the friendly teapot, could cheer her up.

In the dining room, the Beast waited for Belle to join him for dinner.

"Master," said Lumiere, "this girl could be the one to break the spell! You fall in love and . . ."

"She'll always see me as a monster," grumbled the Beast.

Back in the village, Maurice begged for help to rescue Belle from a horrible beast. The crowd laughed, convinced that he was crazy.

But Gaston was thinking up a terrible plan.

At the castle, Belle had skipped dinner and was now hungry.

"Be our guest," said Lumiere, leading Belle to the dining room. Bottles popped their corks, dishes danced, and serving pieces carried in tasty food!

After dinner, Belle wandered into the forbidden west wing and found the enchanted rose.

She was about to touch it when the Beast shouted, "Get out!"

Terrified, Belle fled the castle and rode Philippe into the night.

Spooky yellow eyes glowed in the dark forest.
The wolves were right behind them, lunging at
Philippe's hooves. Belle was thrown off and tumbled
into the snow. The wolf pack surrounded them!

Suddenly, a clawed hand
seized one of the wolves. It
was the Beast!

A wolf bit his arm and the
Beast threw him against a tree.
The pack retreated into the
darkness.

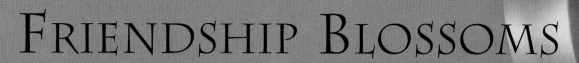

FRIENDSHIP BLOSSOMS

Belle and Philippe helped the injured Beast back to the castle.

Belle tended to the Beast's wound. "Thank you for saving my life," she said gently.

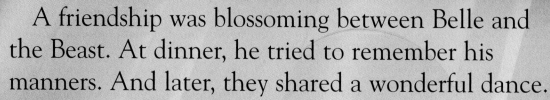

A friendship was blossoming between Belle and the Beast. At dinner, he tried to remember his manners. And later, they shared a wonderful dance. After they danced, the Beast asked Belle if she was happy.

315

"Yes," said Belle. "If only I could see my father."

The Beast brought Belle a magic mirror. When she wished to see her father, Maurice appeared in the glass, wandering lost in the forest.

"You must go to him. Take the mirror with you, so you can remember me," said the Beast sadly.

Belle left the castle. She brought her father home and lovingly cared for him. She told him about the Beast's kindness to her, and how he had let her go. Then there was a knock at the door.

320

Gaston had arrived with an angry crowd. "I'm here to take your crazy father to the asylum. He thinks he's seen a beast." Gaston would only release Maurice if Belle agreed to marry him.

When Belle used the magic mirror to show the Beast to the crowd, Gaston locked Belle and her father in their cellar. He set off to attack the Beast.

When Gaston's mob entered the castle, an army of dishes and furniture assaulted them. Gaston searched the halls until he found the Beast.

At that very moment, Belle escaped from
the cellar and began riding toward the castle!

Just as Belle and her father arrived, Gaston fired an arrow at the Beast.

"No!" sobbed Belle. She charged into the castle and ran up the stairs.

Belle had come back! With new hope, the Beast began to fight. When Belle reached them, the Beast had Gaston by the throat. "Let me go!" cried Gaston. The Beast felt sorry for Gaston and released him.

As the Beast embraced Belle, Gaston stabbed him in the back! The Beast let out a terrible roar, and Gaston tripped and fell off the balcony.

The Beast collapsed in Belle's arms.

"You came back," said the Beast. "At least I got to see you one last time." Belle began to cry. In the Beast's room, the last rose petal was about to fall. "No! Please . . . *please!*" said Belle. "I love you."

331

At Belle's words, the Beast's horrible claws turned into human hands, and his face grew smooth and fine. The spell was broken! "Belle, it's me," said the Prince, and they embraced.

Joyfully, all the enchanted objects in the castle
returned to their human forms.

And as Belle and her prince shared a wonderful
dance, she knew that her dreams of romance and
adventure had all come true.

DISNEP'S

THE
LION KING

✤ RETOLD BY LIZA BAKER ✤

A Prince Is Born

The hot African sun rose on an amazing sight. Giraffes, zebras, elephants, and animals of all kinds were gathered at Pride Rock. This was an important day.

King Mufasa and Queen Sarabi watched as Rafiki, the wise baboon, presented their newborn son to the kingdom. The animals cheered and bowed before Prince Simba.

338

But one family member didn't attend the celebration—Mufasa's brother, Scar. Scar was angry that he was no longer next in line to be king.

Mufasa and his assistant, Zazu, went to ask Scar why he had missed the presentation of Simba.

"Oh, it must have slipped my mind," Scar sneered, and he walked away.

Simba grew into a playful and curious cub. Early one morning, Mufasa brought Simba to the top of Pride Rock. "Everything that the light touches is our kingdom," he told his son. "One day the sun will set on my time here and will rise with you as the new king."

"Wow!" cried Simba. "But what about that shadowy place?"

"You must never go across the border, Simba," said Mufasa sternly.

"But I thought a king can do whatever he wants," said Simba.

Mufasa explained. "There's more to being king than getting your way all the time. You need to respect all creatures. We are all connected in the great Circle of Life."

Simba tried to listen but he was busy chasing grasshoppers and practicing his pounce.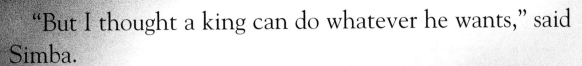

Just then, Zazu arrived with important news. Hyenas had crossed into the Pride Lands!

Mufasa ordered Zazu to take Simba home, and ran off to battle the hyenas.

"I never get to go anywhere," Simba complained.

Back at home, Simba went to see his uncle Scar.
"My dad just showed me the whole kingdom," the cub
bragged. "And I'm gonna rule it all!"

"Did he show you that place beyond the border?" asked
Scar slyly. "Only the bravest of lions would dare go to an
elephant graveyard."

Simba didn't see his uncle's evil trap. He decided to
show his father what a brave cub he could be.

Simba set out to find his best friend, Nala. She was lying with their mothers on a rock nearby. "Mom, can Nala and I go to this great place . . . near the water hole?" fibbed Simba.

"As long as Zazu goes with you," answered Sarabi.

"We've got to ditch Zazu!" Simba whispered to Nala. "We're *really* going to an elephant graveyard!"

Simba and Nala laughed as they ran in and out of animal herds to escape from Zazu. "We lost him!" cried Nala.

Together they played, tumbling and rolling. With a thump, they landed next to a huge elephant skull.

Zazu caught up with them, but it was too late. Banzai, Shenzi, and Ed, three drooling hyenas with sharp teeth, surrounded them!

The hyenas grabbed Zazu first. "Why don't you pick on somebody your own size?" shouted Simba. Then one tried to catch Nala, but Simba swiped his claws across the hyena's cheek.

357

Suddenly, a tremendous roar shook the ground. It was Mufasa!

His giant paw struck one of the hyenas as he growled, "If you ever come near my son again . . ." The hyenas ran away before he could finish.

Mufasa scolded his son on the way home. "You disobeyed me, Simba."

"I was just trying to be brave, like you, Dad," said Simba softly.

"Being brave doesn't mean you go looking for trouble," replied Mufasa.

Then Mufasa told Simba how the kings of the past look down on them from the stars above. "They will always be there to guide you . . . and so will I."

Scar's Trap

Scar was angry when the hyenas told him that Simba had escaped. But he quickly came up with a new plan to get rid of Simba *and* his father.

"I will be king!" he cried.

The next day, Scar found Simba. "Your father has a surprise for you," he said. Scar led Simba down a steep gorge and told him to wait there.

Then Scar signaled the hyenas to frighten a herd of wildebeests. The panicked animals stampeded right toward Simba! Hearing the thunder of hooves, Mufasa looked into the gorge and saw his son. He leaped down and saved Simba's life.

Simba was safe, but Mufasa was still in danger. As he tried to climb away from the stampede, the rocks crumbled beneath him.

Struggling up the cliff, Mufasa saw Scar. "Brother, help me!" he cried.

Scar dug his sharp claws into Mufasa's paws and whispered, "Long live the king!" Then he let Mufasa go, and he disappeared beneath the herd below.

Simba had seen only that his father had fallen. When the stampede was gone, Simba ran to Mufasa. He tried to wake him, but the Lion King was dead.

"Help!" cried Simba.

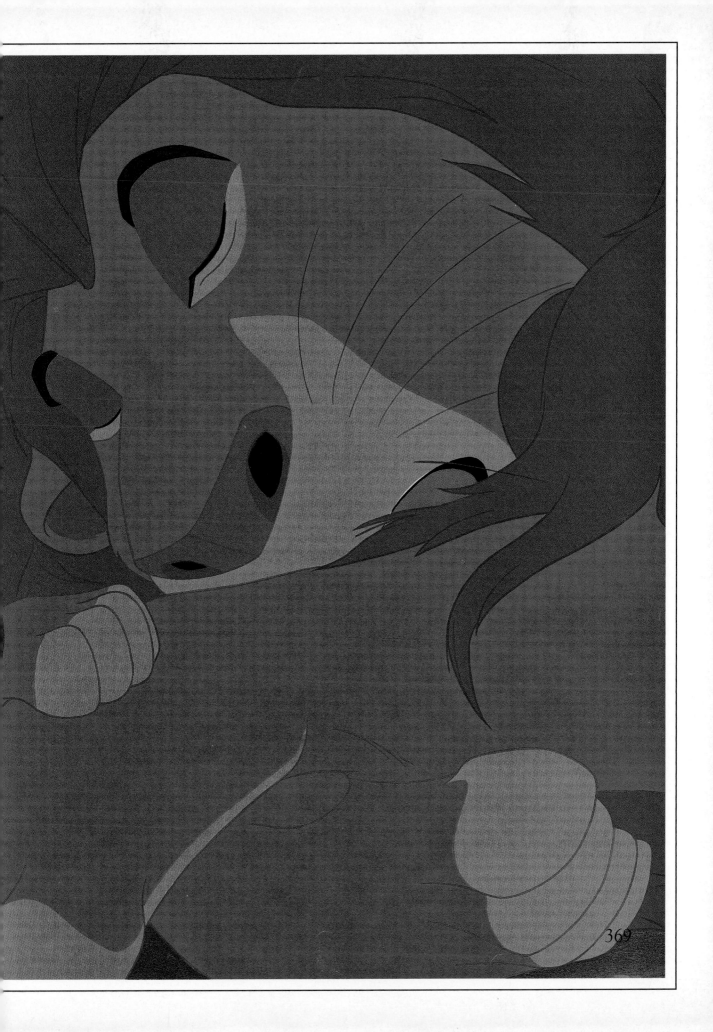

Scar came to Simba's side. "If it weren't for you," he said, "your father would still be alive! Run away and never return!"

Heartbroken, poor Simba ran away as fast as he could.

Scar sent the hyenas out to kill Simba, but the cub escaped them once more.

Scar was certain that Simba was dead. He went back to Pride Rock and told everyone the news. "It is with a heavy heart," he lied, "that I become your new king!"

Everyone in the Pride Lands mourned for their beloved king and Simba.

Meanwhile, Simba was far away from the Pride Lands. The ground turned dry and cracked beneath him. The hot sun beat down as vultures circled above his head.

Exhausted and unable to go any farther, Simba slumped to the ground.

After a long while, Simba awoke. Everything around him looked different. There were trees and grass and flowers instead of desert.

A meerkat named Timon and a warthog named Pumbaa had brought him to their home. "You nearly died," said Pumbaa.

"We saved you!" cried Timon. Thanking them, Simba stood up and started to leave.

Pumbaa asked Simba where he was from, but Simba didn't want to answer. "I did something terrible . . . but I don't want to talk about it."

"You gotta put your troubles behind you, kid," said Timon. "No past, no future, no worries . . . *hakuna matata!*" Simba decided to stay with his new friends.

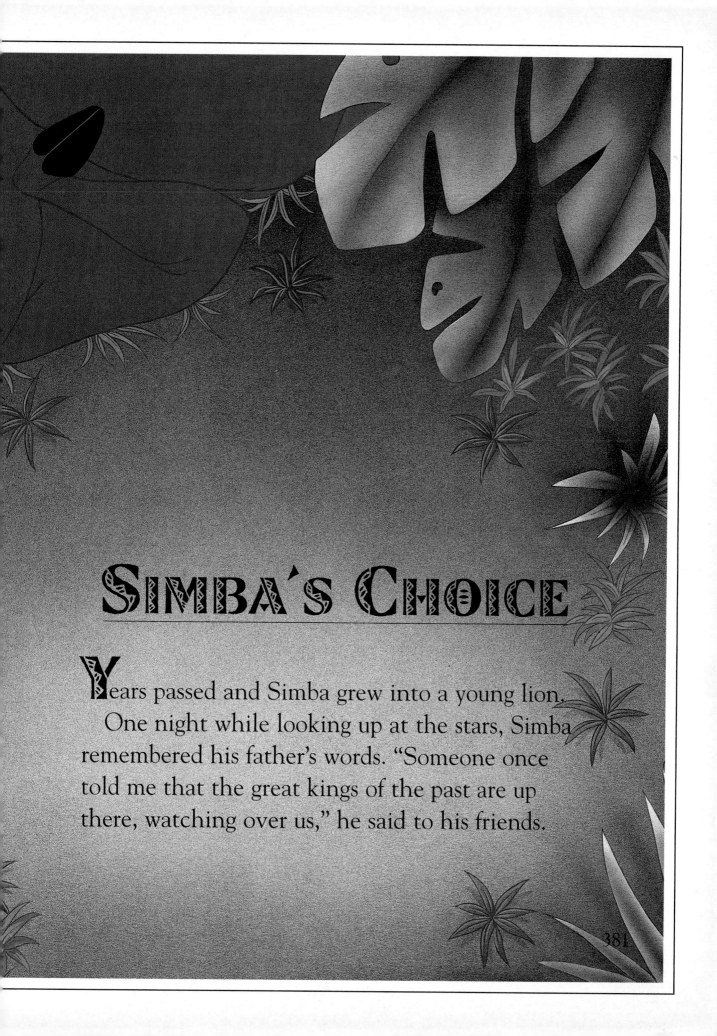

SIMBA'S CHOICE

Years passed and Simba grew into a young lion. One night while looking up at the stars, Simba remembered his father's words. "Someone once told me that the great kings of the past are up there, watching over us," he said to his friends.

The next day, Pumbaa was chasing a bug when a fierce
lioness sprang at him from the tall grass. He screamed and
ran away, but got stuck beneath a fallen tree.

"She's gonna eat me!" he squealed. Simba heard his
friend's cries and rushed to help.

383

Simba wrestled with the lioness, but then realized she was his old friend Nala. "You're alive!" she said happily. "That means you're the king!"

Nala told Simba how Scar had destroyed the Pride Lands. "Simba, if you don't do something, everyone will starve."

"I can't go back," said Simba angrily, and he turned and walked away.

Simba thought about what Nala had said.
"I *won't* go back," he said to himself. "It won't
change anything." Just then, Simba heard a
chanting song from the jungle.

Rafiki the baboon came walking
toward him. "If you want to see your
father again, look down there,"
Rafiki said, pointing into the
pool of water next to them.

388

Simba saw the face of his father staring back at him. "You see?" said Rafiki. "He lives in you!"

Now Simba looked up and saw his father's face in the stars and heard his voice. "Look inside yourself, Simba. Remember who you are . . . you are my son and the one true king."

The next morning Rafiki found Nala, Timon, and Pumbaa. He told them that Simba had returned to the Pride Lands. "He's gone back to challenge his uncle!" cheered Nala.

When Simba reached the Pride Lands, he was saddened by what he saw. His homeland that was once green and beautiful had turned barren under Scar's rule. Bravely, Simba continued on his journey.

When Simba arrived at Pride Rock, he let out a roar that shook the earth. Scar was surprised and frightened. He thought the hyenas had killed Simba long ago.

"This is my kingdom!" shouted Simba. "Step down, Scar." Scar ordered his hyenas to attack. They surrounded Simba and drove him to the edge of a cliff.

Simba grabbed onto the rocks with his claws as Scar stood above him. "That's just the way your father looked before I killed him," snarled Scar.

Then Simba realized that it had been Scar who killed his father. With new strength, Simba lunged onto the rock and attacked.

At that moment, Nala, Timon, and Pumbaa arrived and a battle broke out on Pride Rock.

This time, Simba trapped Scar at the steep edge of Pride Rock. Sparing his life, he ordered his uncle to run away and never return.

Scar pretended to leave, but then turned and lunged at Simba. Simba swiped his great claw and Scar fell to his death in the gorge below.

Simba took his rightful place as the Lion King and once again the land flourished. Soon all the animals gathered at Pride Rock to celebrate the birth of Simba and Nala's cub. The Circle of Life would continue.